Enid Blyton's

All the Way to Sant

ILLUSTRATED BY PAMELA VENUS

A TEMPLAR BOOK

Produced by The Templar Company plc, Pippbrook Mill, London Road, Dorking, Surrey RH4 1JE

This edition produced for Parragon Book Service Ltd, Unit 13-17, Avonbridge Trading Estate, Atlantic Road, Avonmouth, Bristol BS11 9QD

This book contains material first published as *All the Way to Santa Claus* in The Seventh Holiday Book
by Samson, Marston & Co Ltd 1953.

Printed and bound in Great Britain

ISBN 0-75251-078-9

It was nearly Christmas time, and Santa Claus and all his helpers were very busy making thousands of toys in the workshop below Santa's castle.

Tops were humming, rocking horses were rocking, trains were rattling round and round on their rails, and teddy bears were practising their growls. The toy makers were working very hard, and everywhere you went there were toys being made, ready for Christmas.

Now one of the little workers was a brownie called Slick. He was the one that taught the jack-in-the-boxes to pop up on their springs and make people jump. Nobody liked him very much. He didn't always tell the truth, and he liked nothing better than to play tricks on people.

"I don't trust him," said one brownie to another. "And I wish he would go away." But Santa Claus overheard and told the brownies not to be nasty. Little did Santa know that Slick was planning a very nasty trick indeed. He had decided to steal the sack of toys that Santa Claus was going to take out with him on Christmas Eve!

P. VENUS

Now, this sack was a magic sack. It looked as if it could hold only a hundred toys, but it could really hold as many toys as Santa needed to give away on Christmas Eve!

Slick had asked Mr. Hessian, who made a new sack for Santa every year, how he managed to fit all the toys into one sack.

“It’s easy!” said Mr. Hessian, who was busy sewing some magic into every stitch.

“On Christmas Eve Santa blows a whistle, and all the toys come to life. Then they march out of their different toy rooms in a long line, and walk straight into the sack. It doesn’t matter how many there are, they can all fit in. Then Santa Claus ties up the neck of the sack, and goes off with it in his sledge.”

That was all that Slick wanted to know. Now he knew just what to do!

"I'll pretend that there is to be a *practice* march into the sack this year," he said to himself. "And *I'll* be the one to blow the whistle and hold the sack open for the toys to march in! Then I'll tie it up and use one of the toy cars to take me to the Land of Boys and Girls. I'll sell the toys to all the toyshops there and make a lot of money! What a splendid trick that will be!"

So, one night when all the other brownies were asleep, Slick told all the toys that there was to be a practice march into the sack.

"When I blow my whistle, you must all come quickly," he said.

He blew his whistle and at once the teddy bears got up and marched, growling, into the sack. The ducks waddled and quacked, and the dolls walked in. The trains rushed in at top speed and so did the toy cars. The balls rolled along, the tops spun there and even the bricks hopped, skipped or jumped along. As for the toy soldiers, they marched smartly in a line behind their captain. It really was a sight to see.

"It's only a practice march," whispered the dolls. "We shan't be in this smelly sack very long!"

But, to their great dismay, Slick tightly tied up the neck of the sack and began to drag it along the floor to the back door, where he had his car waiting! Nobody heard the toys crying out for help. It really was very easy for Slick to steal them all.

In two minutes the big castle was quiet again. No growling, clattering, rocking, or quacking disturbed the silence, for not a toy was left. They were all crowded together in the magic sack, being driven off to be sold in toyshops in the Land of Boys and Girls.

The captain of the soldiers soon guessed that something was wrong. He shouted out to Slick.

"Hey! What are you doing with us? Where are you taking us? Let us out! I shall complain to Santa Claus!"

Slick laughed loudly. "You'll never see *him* again. Just imagine what the children will say when they find out that Santa Claus hasn't any toys to give them for Christmas!"

The toys were frightened and upset. They all began to talk at once and the tops hummed so loudly that it was difficult to hear what was being said.

"Silence!" shouted the captain of the toy soldiers. "I have a plan. Please listen carefully, all of you."

When the toys stopped making a noise, the captain spoke in a quiet voice.

"We need to find our way back to Santa Claus as soon as possible," he said. "It is nearly Christmas Eve and if we don't return, there will be no presents for Santa to take to the children. I have a sharp sword, and I am going to cut a hole in the side of the sack. My soldiers and I will escape through the hole. Once we are out, you must follow us and we will lead you back to the castle!"

Then, taking his sharp sword, the brave captain cut a large hole in the sack.

Out he marched with his soldiers close behind, and they found themselves at the back of the car. It was not going very fast, because there was snow on the ground, and Slick was driving very slowly in case he skidded.

One by one the soldiers climbed out of the car, and silently dropped down onto the snowy ground. All the toys followed them as quietly as they could. Soon the sack was quite empty but Slick didn't know that. Oh, no! He drove on, thinking that he still had hundreds of toys behind him!

The toys looked around them. It was evening and they were on the outskirts of a big town. They wondered what they should do next.

"There's a policeman!" whispered a big doll. "Shall we ask him the way back to Santa Claus?"

So the toys made their way in a long line, over the snow, to the policeman. But when he saw this strange collection of tiny things moving towards him, he thought he must be seeing things and ran away back to the police station.

"He's run away," said the captain crossly. "Now what shall we do?" Just then one of the teddy bears cried out, "Look – there's somebody else coming up the road – two people. Oh, they're children!"

Sure enough, two children were trudging along in the snowy night. The soldiers followed their captain to a lamp-post, and there the children saw them, a long line of little shining toys.

"Look, Sophie – toy soldiers – and oh, my goodness, there are dolls too – and toy bears and pandas – lots of them. Are we dreaming?"

"We must be, James," said Sophie. "But it's a lovely dream. Listen – this little soldier is speaking to us!"

"Do you know the way to Santa's castle?" the captain was asking, in a high, squeaky voice. "Somebody stole us away from there tonight, and we want to go back."

Well, of course, Sophie and James made the same answer that *you* would have made.

"We don't know! We know he lives in a castle somewhere in a snowy land where reindeer live, but we couldn't possibly tell you the way!"

"Oh, dear! What are we going to do? We really *must* get back!" said a big doll. "It's almost Christmas time and we're the toys that Santa Claus puts into children's stockings! We're not shop toys, you know."

"Perhaps a reindeer could tell us the way," said the captain. "All reindeer know the way to the land of Santa Claus. Do you have a pet reindeer that we could ask?"

P.VENUS.

"No!" said Sophie, with a laugh. "But there are reindeer at the zoo, and that's not very far from here."

"Could you please take us there?" asked the captain. "Maybe the reindeer can help us find the way."

"The zoo is closed now," said James. "But we could take you to the gates, and as you are so small you could easily slip through the railings."

"I don't know how to thank you," said the captain. "I shall tell Santa Claus all about you when we get back, and I will ask him to bring you some special toys this Christmas, as a reward for your help."

"What are your names?" asked the big doll, as they all walked down the street through the snow.

"I'm James and my sister is Sophie," said James. "This *is* a funny thing to happen! I still wonder if I'm dreaming!"

After some time they came to the gates of the big zoo, and the toys slipped through the railings. They called goodbye to

Sophie and James and went into the dark zoo. They heard a wolf howling, and they heard owls hooting. And then they smelt the familiar smell of reindeer! The captain sniffed hard.

"I can smell them," he said. "Their house must be somewhere near here. Come along."

So, through the zoo, along the snowy paths, went a long, long line of toys, much to the surprise of the zoo animals.

At last the toys came to the reindeer house. The reindeer were fast asleep. There were two of them, and the captain gently prodded them until they woke up with a jump.

"Who's that?" said one reindeer.

"Excuse me please, reindeer, but do you know where Santa Claus lives?" asked the captain.

"Of course," said the reindeer. "I used to live not far from his castle. I always hoped I'd be chosen to draw his sledge at Christmas, but I never was. I even practised galloping through the sky, like his sledge reindeer do. But I wasn't fast enough. Why do you want to know?"

"Well, we are all Christmas toys, and somebody stole us from Santa Claus's castle," said the captain. "But we escaped. And now we want to go back. Could you please, please, tell us the way?"

"Well, you want to go the sky-way – it's much quicker than any other way," said the reindeer. "Can you see that big star there? Well, you go straight towards that, but at midnight you steer by those three stars to the right … and …"

The listening toys groaned. None of them knew how to fly through the sky. But just at that moment one of the teddy bears had a brilliant idea.

"Reindeer, you know how to gallop through the air, don't you? Could you *possibly* take us on your back, do you think? Santa Claus would be so grateful to you."

"What a good idea!" said the first reindeer, beginning to get excited. And soon the two of them had agreed to help the toys.

First the reindeer had to remember the spell that was used for galloping in the sky. Then they decided that it would be wise to practise for a bit first, for neither of them had flown for many years. As they muttered the magic words, the reindeer began to rise up and up into the air, while the toys watched from below.

They flew round and round practising, and it wasn't long before they felt confident enough to land and pick up the toys. One of the zoo keepers looked up and saw the reindeer in the sky, but he didn’t believe what he was seeing.

“There must be something wrong with my eyes,” he said, shaking his head. “Reindeer in the sky, indeed! Why, I’ll be believing in Santa Claus next!” Chuckling he went back into his office and didn’t do anything about them at all, which was a very good thing.

Gently the reindeer glided to a halt in front of the toys.

“All aboard,” they said and the toys climbed on to the reindeer’s backs – and not only on to their backs, but on their necks and noses and even their tails! There were so very many toys, you see.

They all managed to get on at last and then – off they went! It was so exciting to be galloping through the sky.

The toys had to hang on tightly because the reindeer went so fast. They flew high over snow-covered fields and villages and at last they arrived at the castle of Santa Claus. The reindeer stamped up the steps puffing and blowing and feeling very important.

The castle door opened and down the steps came Santa Claus. All his workers followed him looking very surprised. They were so pleased to see that all the toys had come back.

"Where have you been toys?" cried Santa Claus. "Who are these fine reindeer?"

The toys crowded round Santa all trying to speak at once.

"Ssh," said Santa, laughing. "One at a time. I can't understand what you are saying."

The captain of the toy soldiers stepped forward and told Santa Claus all about their adventure. There was such an excited humming and squeaking and growling all around that Santa Claus could hardly hear.

"That naughty Slick!" he cried. "But he'll be sorry when he realises that he's stuck in the Land of Girls and Boys. I shall only let him back when he's mended his wicked ways. Now, I must reward Sophie and James, and these two reindeer. What reward would you like?"

"Oh, please, Santa Claus, *may* we help to draw your sledge on Christmas Eve?" asked the reindeer. "We could gallop here from the zoo."

"All right!" said Santa Claus. "Come along here on Christmas Eve at eight o'clock, so that I can get you ready. And now – what about these children, Sophie and James? I'd better take them some extra special presents, I think. Where do they live, captain?"

Well, would you believe it, nobody knew!

"I forgot to ask for their address," said the captain. "And I don't know their surnames, either. Oh dear, how will you reward Sophie and James now, Santa Claus?"

"I'll have to look in my special Christmas book for *all* the children named Sophie and James," said Santa Claus, "and I'll leave *all* of them some extra special toys. That's the only thing I can do! Now come along to bed, all of you. You must be very tired."

Well, that is the story of how all the Christmas toys were stolen, and how they got back safely to Santa Claus. I hope your name is Sophie or James, because if it is, you'll be very lucky this year, won't you?